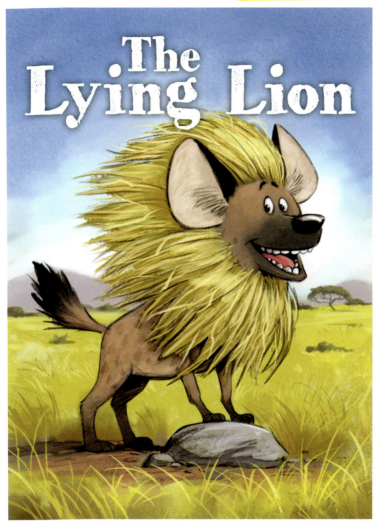

The Lying Lion

By Megan Hoyt, M.A.
Illustrated by Howard McWilliam

Consultant

Chrissy Johnson, M.Ed.
Second Grade Teacher
Cedar Point Elementary School, Virginia

Publishing Credits

Rachelle Cracchiolo, M.S.Ed., *Publisher*
Emily R. Smith, M.A.Ed., *VP of Content Development*
Véronique Bos, *Creative Director*
Dani Neiley, *Associate Editor*
Kevin Pham, *Graphic Designer*

Image Credits

Illustrated by Howard McWilliam

Library of Congress Cataloging-in-Publication Data

Names: Hoyt, Megan, author. | McWilliam, Howard, 1977- illustrator.
Title: The lying lion / by Megan Hoyt, M.A. ; illustrated by Howard
　McWilliam.
Description: Huntington Beach, CA : Teacher Created Materials, [2022] |
　Audience: Grades 2-3. | Summary: "Henry Hyena wants to find his place in
　the world. But who wants to be a silly little hyena? He decides he wants
　to be a lion. He wants amazing pouncing skills and a full mane. What
　will he do when he comes face-to-face with the king of the jungle?"--
　Provided by publisher.
Identifiers: LCCN 2022003582 (print) | LCCN 2022003583 (ebook) | ISBN
　9781087605340 (paperback) | ISBN 9781087632209 (ebook)
Subjects: LCSH: Readers (Primary) | LCGFT: Readers (Publications)
Classification: LCC PE1119.2 .H795 2022 (print) | LCC PE1119.2 (ebook) |
　DDC 428.6/2--dc23/eng/20220206
LC record available at https://lccn.loc.gov/2022003582
LC ebook record available at https://lccn.loc.gov/2022003583

5482 Argosy Avenue
Huntington Beach, CA 92649
www.tcmpub.com

ISBN 978-1-0876-0534-0

Table of Contents

Chapter 1

─────•●•─────

BUGS FOR BREAKFAST

Henry Hyena stepped out of his dark, cozy den and into bright sunlight for the first time. He blinked and yawned and stretched. The world was so big!

His sisters scurried out in a crowded pack, leaving a trail of dust. It made Henry cough and sputter.

"Time for breakfast!" Mother said.

"Beetles, grubs, and flies?" Henry asked.

His sisters gobbled up the tasty bugs. But Henry just stared at his food, longing for something to really sink his teeth into.

He gazed at the horizon and could see a pride of lions chomping on thick, juicy meat.

"Yum!" Henry said.

"I'm glad you're enjoying your first big breakfast, Henry," Mother said, smiling.

Henry tore his eyes away from the pride. He gave his mother a small smile. He wanted her to know he was grateful for the breakfast she had prepared. But he would have much rather been eating meat.

Playtime with his sisters was nothing but games and giggles. But Henry wanted to do something wilder.

Henry wanted to rumble. He wanted to wrestle and run and ramble across the savanna. His sisters didn't, and they were happy to have fun without Henry. He felt lonely and sad. He couldn't get the lions he saw earlier out of his mind.

I know! Henry thought to himself. *If I smear this dust on my spots to hide them and make a mane out of these prickly weeds, I'll look just like a lion.*

He laughed a high, shrill, piercing laugh. It was the kind of laugh only a happy, young hyena can make. Henry felt very giddy now and very powerful, like a lion!

Suddenly, he was surrounded by his silly sisters with their perfect spots and smooth fur. They laughed hysterically at Henry.

"You sounded like a foghorn!" one sister exclaimed.

"No, it was more like an elephant!" another shouted.

Henry clutched the dry, cracked weeds tightly in his paw and let out a mournful howl. *Tomorrow, I will become a lion*, he thought.

Chapter 2

The Itchy, Twitchy Mane

Henry Hyena woke up early and tiptoed across the quiet plain. The lions were practicing their hunting with leaps and pounces. Leon was the fastest, strongest, and biggest of the pride. Henry thought he was the bravest, too.

Oh, if only I could pounce and race like Leon, he thought. *No one would laugh at me if I were the bravest lion on the savanna!*

Henry pulled handfuls of dry grass off the ground. He began tying them to the fur on his head.

He kept at his work until his entire face was wrapped in sticks and dry grass. He even tied some grass to his tail, trying to make it longer so he would look just like a member of the lion pride. But all the grass made it hard to run. Henry awkwardly stumbled across the field. He held his head high and tried to swish his new tail with confidence.

"I am King of the Savanna!" he exclaimed.

But he was not the King of the Savanna.
He was only a young hyena, still learning
how to run and leap, so the grass on his tail
tripped him and came untied. Then, he
was tumbling across the ground. All he saw
as he tumbled was sky, land, sky, land. He
came to a stop and shook off the dizziness.
When he opened his eyes, he found himself
right in the middle of the lions' hunting
practice. To his horror, he was eye to eye
with the bravest, strongest lion of all.

"Hello, little one!" Leon rumbled. "Where did you tumble in from?"

He brushed the sticks away from Henry's face and chuckled.

"Oh! You're not a lion at all! You're a hyena," he said.

All the other lions rolled around on the dusty ground, roaring with laughter. Henry had never been so embarrassed. He got up and ran home as fast as his legs would carry him.

As he ran, he thought about what had happened. How could he ever join the pride looking so tiny and spotted and frightened? Maybe if he tried joining the pride at night, they would not be able to see that he was a hyena. But they *would* be able to hear him. He would have to practice his roaring until he could blend in with the other cubs.

Chapter Three

—•—●—•—

READY TO RUMBLE

Henry practiced his roar until nightfall. It was almost time to join the lion pride.

"Raaaawr-hee-hee!" No, that wasn't quite right.

"Roar-ee-ee-ee!" No, that wasn't it either. No matter how hard he tried to roar, Henry ended up laughing.

Ray Rhino strolled by. "Hi, Henry!" he said.

Henry roared. "I'm not Henry!" he said.

"Well, you are no lion!" Ray said.

"Holy hyenas! How did you know it was me?" Henry asked.

"Your voice," Ray answered. "It's unmistakable!"

Henry and Ray peeked through the tall grass at the practicing pride.

"Lions are awesome!" Henry said with a sigh.

"Hyenas are awesome, too," Ray said.

"No, we're not! We're spotted and striped, and we lumber along, stumbling over our own feet. I'm surprised we ever find enough food to eat. We're not even half as fast as those lions. And look!"

Mama Lion was preparing that delicious meat *again*. Henry's mouth began to water. His heart sunk to his toes. Then, he let out the most mournful wail the animals of the savanna had ever heard.

Ray tried to stifle his laughter, but it came bursting out in huge snorts. "Ha-ha-ha! Why don't you want to be a hyena?" he asked. "You are hilarious!"

"I'll show you!" Henry said. He let out the most monstrous mournful sound. Not even a lion cub would make such a sad noise. Henry Hyena was pitiful.

Once Henry's eyes adjusted to the darkness, he saw that all the animals of the savanna were gathered around him. They were pointing and laughing.

Zebras whistled and whinnied. "What *are* you trying to do?"

Snakes coiled and hissed. "Sssssomething is quite wrong here."

Meerkats hopped and chattered. "Tee-hee-hee! That's funny!"

Worst of all, his sisters were loping across the field in the moonlight far away. Their laughter could be heard for miles and miles.

It seemed the whole world was laughing at the poor little hyena with the terrible roar. But one animal was not.

Leon Lion was scouring the savanna, looking for a morsel to eat. The hyena sisters seemed like a most delicious dinner!

Henry's night vision kicked in and he saw the danger.

His chest rumbled.

His throat tickled.

Something was growing deep within his hyena heart.

It was not a silly laugh.

It was not a mournful cry.

It was something much more powerful.

It was a giant ROAR! And it came bursting from him as naturally as if he were a lion!

"STOP!" he roared.

All the animals froze. Then, they scattered in surprise. They tumbled across the field, yapping and squeaking, hissing and honking.

Only one remained.

Chapter Four

The Heart of the Matter

Leon, King of the Savanna, took a deep breath and quietly growled, "*You* are *not* a lion."

"I may not be a lion, but I am courageous just the same!" Henry cried.

Leon roared so loudly that Henry's mouth went dry and his tail drooped.

"I *am* courageous!" Henry whispered to himself.

While Leon was busy talking to Henry, Mother and Father returned from the hunt with only beetles and worms again.

When they saw Leon, they gathered their daughters and rushed back to their den. Then, Mother peeked out and spotted Henry. He was standing face-to-face with the king of beasts.

"Holy hyenas!" she said. "It's our Henry, and he's in danger!"

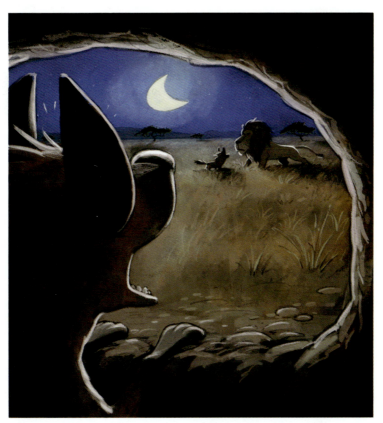

Henry swallowed hard.

His breath came in rapid pants.

His heart pounded.

His paws shook.

"I know you win every race and have a ton of fans. But you will never outwit a courageous hyena like me," he said.

"So, you admit you are a hyena!" Leon said. "No more lying. If you really think you deserve to join our pride, then you have to decide. Are you going to be a truthful hyena or a lying lion? You can never go back to your hyena pack if you decide to join us. But you're OK with that, right, lion?"

"I am a hyena, through and through!" Henry said. "Even if I have to eat beetles and worms every day for the rest of my life!"

Henry ran as fast as his loping legs would carry him. He ran across the prairie, past the bushes, through the crackling weeds. He ran until he was home.

The moment Henry slid into the den, his parents and sisters cheered.

"You are a hero, Henry!" Mother said, smiling proudly.

"You saved our lives!" one sister gushed.

"You are as brave as a lion!" another exclaimed.

Henry looked at his loving family. He looked at his meager meal of bugs and flies and smiled. He did not need a meat dinner. He did not need the approval of a pride of lions to feel good about who he was. He was meant to be a happy hyena. That meant there would be no more lying, no more itchy, tickly costumes, and no more roaring!

"I am Henry Hyena, prince of the pack!" he said, standing tall and proud.

That night was full of games and giggles. This time, Henry yipped and howled and giggled right along with his sisters, like only young hyenas do.

"Ha-ha-ha-ha-hee! Ha-ha-ha-ha-hoo! We are hyenas, through and through!"

About Us

The Author

Megan Hoyt is an award-winning children's picture book author and poet. She lives in Charlotte, North Carolina, with her husband and two fluffy dogs. One of them is tiny, and one thinks he is big (like Henry Hyena).

The Illustrator

Howard McWilliam is the cover artist for *The Week* in the United Kingdom and United States and has illustrated many children's books, including John Cena's Elbow Grease series and the bestselling I Need My Monster books. He left his career as a financial magazine editor and journalist in 2005 to concentrate on illustrating. He lives in Cheltenham, England, with his wife and three young sons.